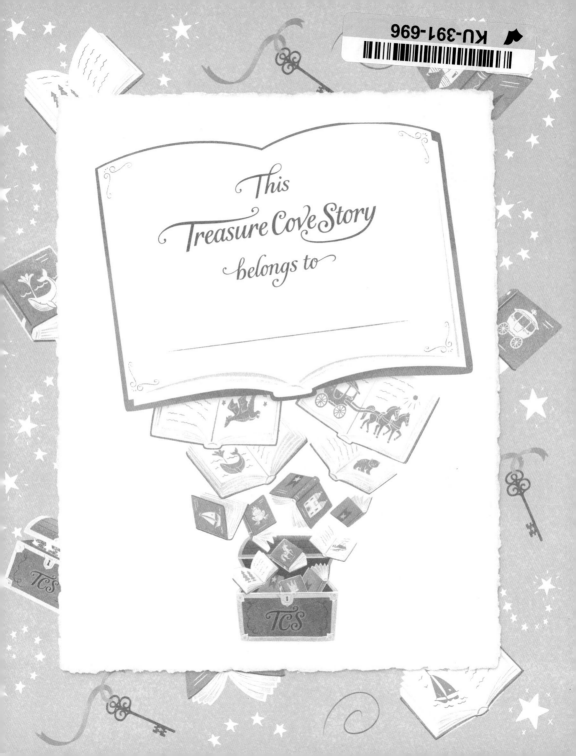

This
Treasure Cove Story
belongs to

THE THREAT OF THANOS

A CENTUM BOOK 978-1-912841-39-4
Published in Great Britain by Centum Books Ltd.
This edition published 2019.

3 5 7 9 10 8 6 4 2

Centum Books Ltd, 20 Devon Square, Newton Abbot, Devon, TQ12 2HR, UK.
9/10 Fenian St, Dublin 2, D02 RX24, Ireland.

www.centumbooksltd.co.uk | books@centumbooksltd.co.uk
CENTUM BOOKS Limited Reg. No. 07641486.

A CIP catalogue record for this book is available
from the British Library.

Printed in China.

MARVEL
AVENGERS

The THREAT of THANOS

By Arie Kaplan
Illustrated by Shane Clester

Earth's mightiest heroes, the **Avengers**, had been called to a laboratory in New York City, where scientists were studying a purple gem from outer space.

'It's giving off strange ᴇɴᴇʀɢʏ ᴡᴀᴠᴇs...
almost like it's sending a message,' Iron Man said.

'But who's it calling?' Wasp asked.

Suddenly, a portal opened and a fearsome figure appeared! He wore a **GOLDEN GAUNTLET** on one hand.

Black Panther growled.

THANOS!

'That gem is the final **Infinity Stone**,' Thanos
declared. 'It is calling out to the other stones. With
all six of them, I can **RULE THE UNIVERSE**!'

The heroes leaped into action,
ready to stop him.

'Avengers, **mind** your own business,'
the villain growled.

An invisible force pushed the heroes back!
'How did he *do* that?' Black Panther asked.

'Thanos is using the **Mind Stone**,' Iron Man
explained. 'It lets him push people around with just
his **thoughts**.'

With the Avengers out of the way, Thanos grabbed the **purple gem**. He put it into his gauntlet, and the golden glove started to **glow**.

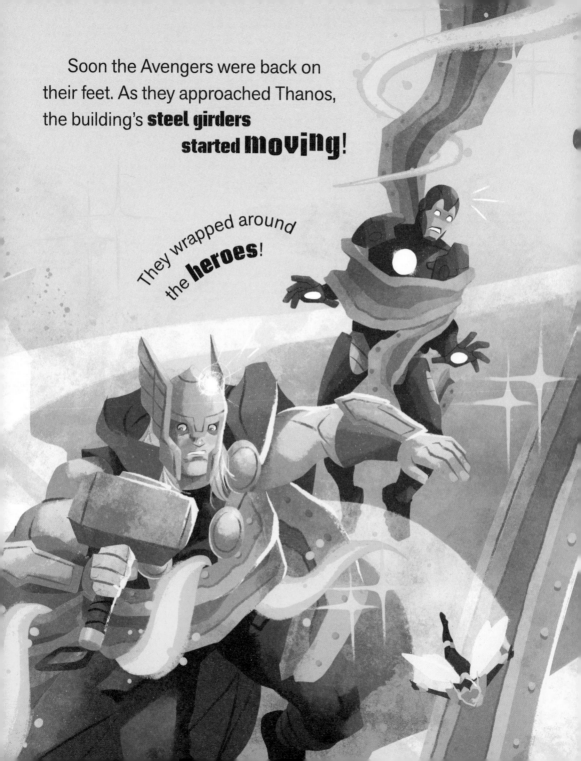

Soon the Avengers were back on their feet. As they approached Thanos, the building's **steel girders** started **moving**!

They wrapped around the **heroes**!

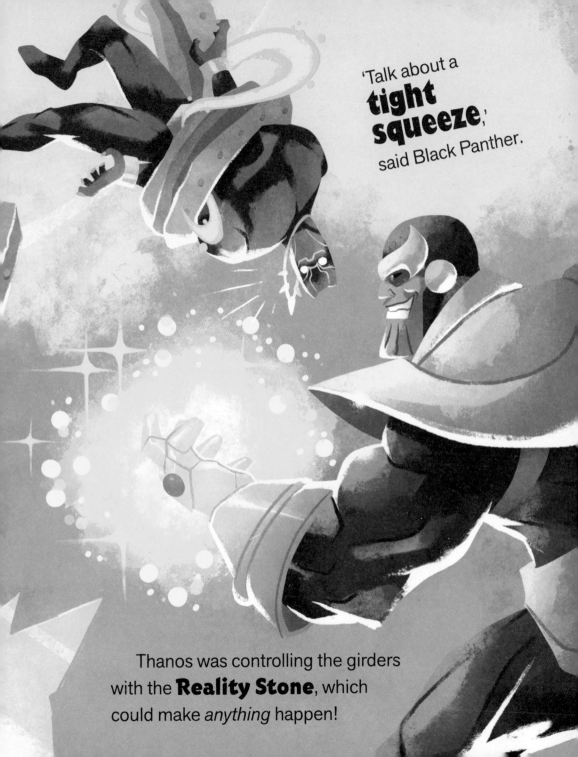

'Talk about a **tight squeeze**,' said Black Panther.

Thanos was controlling the girders with the **Reality Stone**, which could make *anything* happen!

Iron Man used his powerful suit of armour to burst free.

Thor smashed the girders with his hammer.

Black Panther *sliced* through the steel with his *claws*.

And Wasp was too small and too fast to get caught.

Then the heroes tackled Thanos. But they couldn't remove his gauntlet!

Thanos zapped the heroes with bolts of alien energy.

Earth's Mightiest Heroes
fell to the ground.

'That was like getting
hit with the world's biggest
flyswatter!' Wasp joked.

'I'm feeling greedy,' Thanos said to Thor. 'I came here for the **gem**. But I think I'll *also* take your **hammer**!'

'You are not **worthy** to lift my mighty hammer,'
Thor said weakly. 'Still, I dare you to **try**!'

Thanos grabbed the hammer, and Thor smiled. The blond hero reached out his hand and the magic hammer returned to him.

It flew so quickly, it pulled the Infinity Gauntlet
right off the villain's hand!

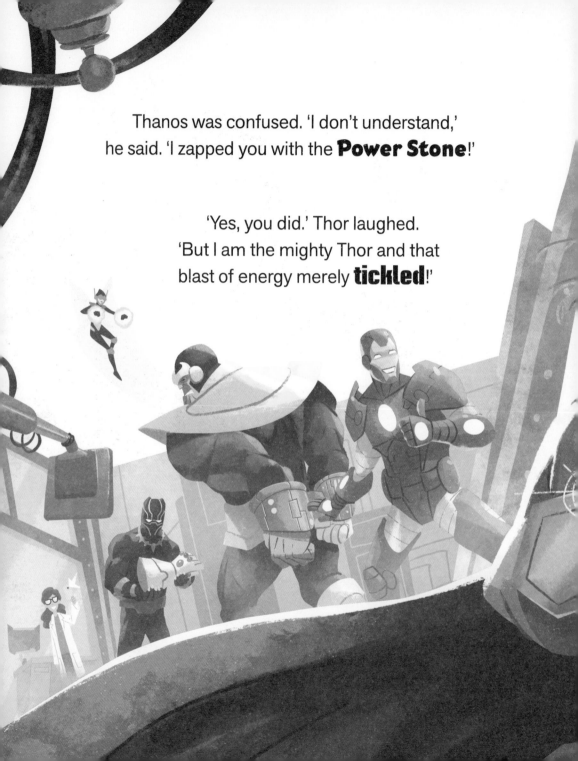

Thanos was confused. 'I don't understand,' he said. 'I zapped you with the **Power Stone**!'

'Yes, you did.' Thor laughed. 'But I am the mighty Thor and that blast of energy merely **tickled**!'

With Thanos under the Avengers' control,
Iron Man contacted an interplanetary police force
called the **NOVA CORPS**.

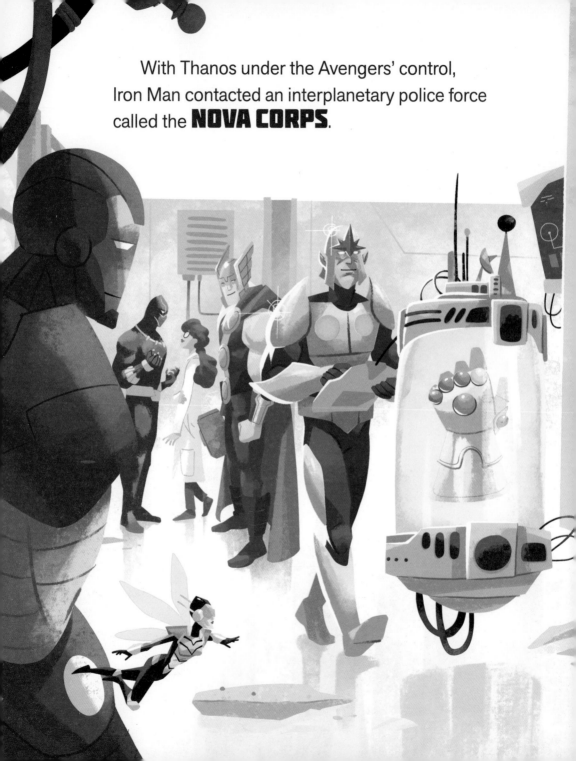

Nova Corps officers soon arrived to take Thanos away to an alien prison.

'We will put the Infinity Gauntlet in a safe place,' the officers promised.

With the day saved, the Avengers headed home.
'Thanos was trying to complete his collection of
Infinity Stones,' Black Panther said to his friends.
'But he was no match for *this* collection of heroes!'

Treasure Cove Stories

Please contact Centum Books to receive the full list of titles in the *Treasure Cove Stories* series.
books@centumbooksltd.co.uk

Book list may be subject to change. Not all titles are listed.